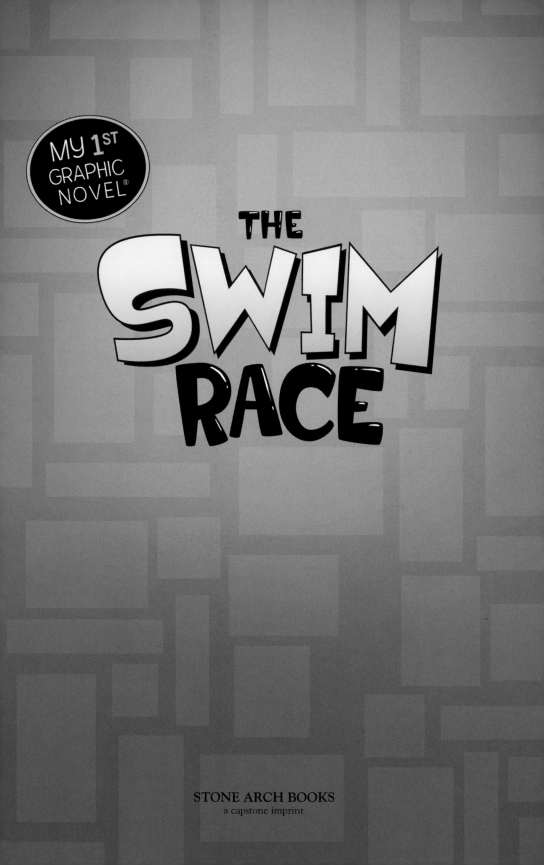

MY 1ST GRAPHIC NOVEL®

THE SWIM RACE

STONE ARCH BOOKS
a capstone imprint

My First Graphic Novels are published by Stone Arch Books
A Capstone Imprint
1710 Roe Crest Drive, North Mankato, Minnesota 56003
www.capstonepub.com

Library of Congress Cataloging-in-Publication Data
Yasuda, Anita.
The swim race / by Anita Yasuda; illustrated by Steve Harpster.
p. cm. — (My first graphic novel)
Summary: Casey really enjoys her swimming class at the sports center and imagines her first race.
ISBN 978-1-4342-3280-9 (library binding)
ISBN 978-1-4342-3864-1 (pbk.)
1. Swimming—Comic books, strips, etc. 2. Swimming—Juvenile fiction. 3. Graphic novels. [1. Graphic novels. 2. Swimming—Fiction. 3. Imagination—Fiction.] I. Harpster, Steve, ill. II. Title. III. Series: My first graphic novel.
PZ7.7.Y37Sw 2012
741.5'973—dc23

2011032215

Art Director: Bob Lentz
Graphic Designer: Brann Garvey
Production Specialist: Michelle Biedscheid

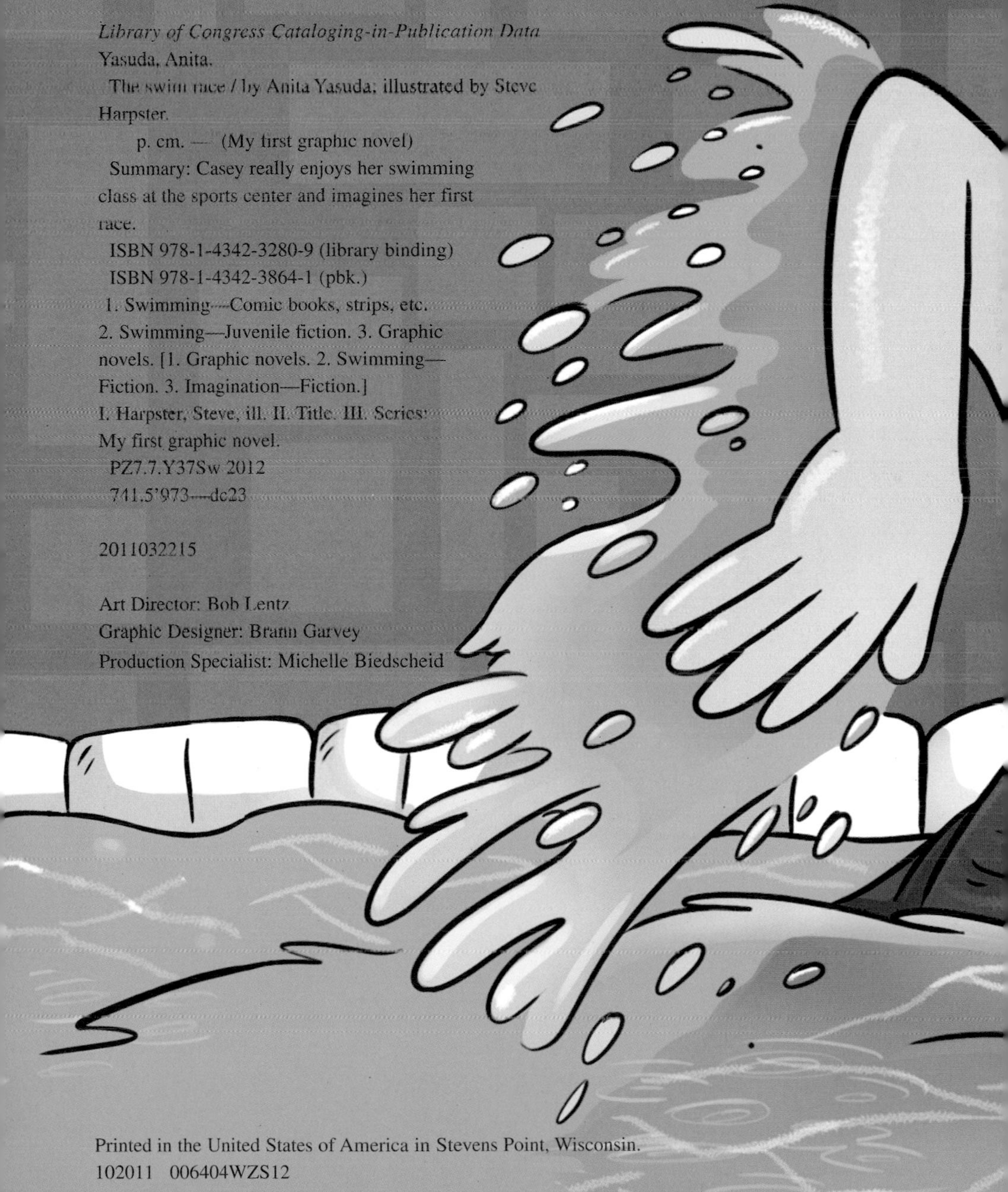

Printed in the United States of America in Stevens Point, Wisconsin.
102011 006404WZS12

THE SWIM RACE

written by
Anita Yasuda

illustrated by
Steve Harpster

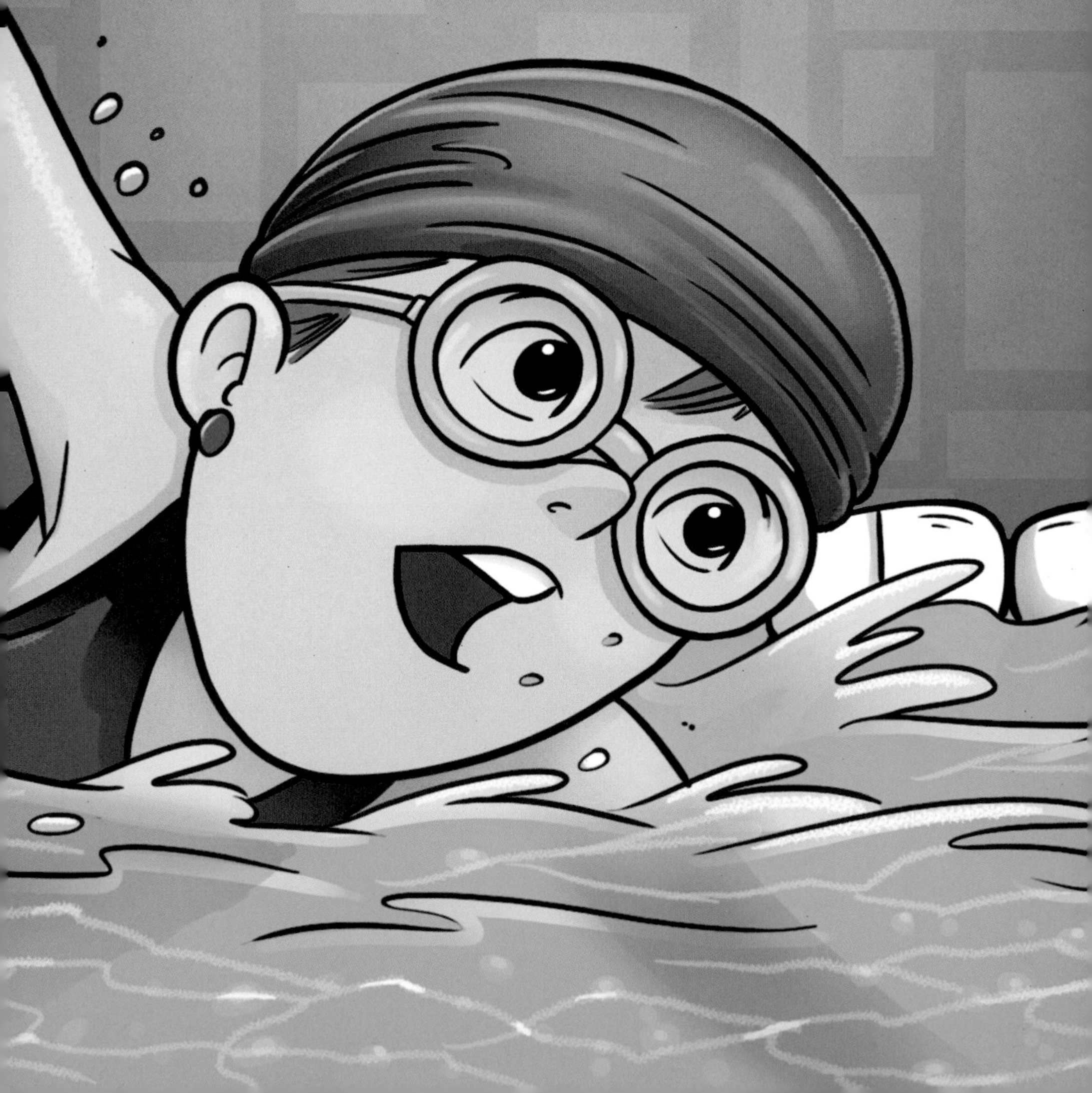

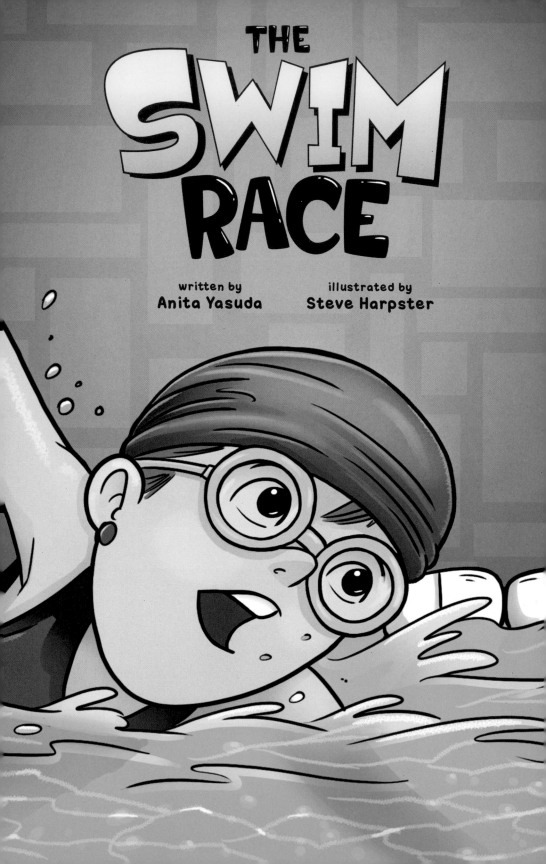

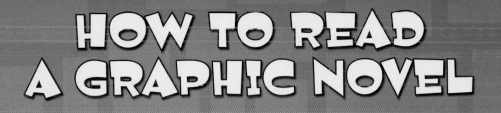

HOW TO READ A GRAPHIC NOVEL

Graphic novels are easy to read. Boxes called panels show you how to follow the story. Look at the panels from left to right and top to bottom.

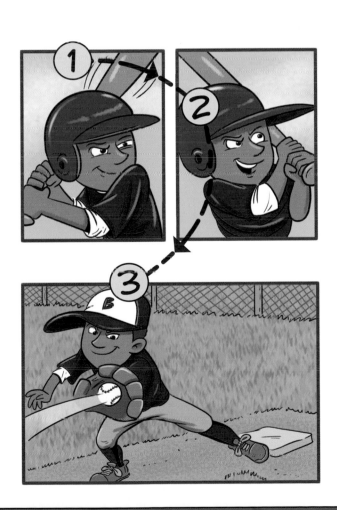

Read the word boxes and word balloons from left to right as well. Don't forget the sound and action words in the pictures.

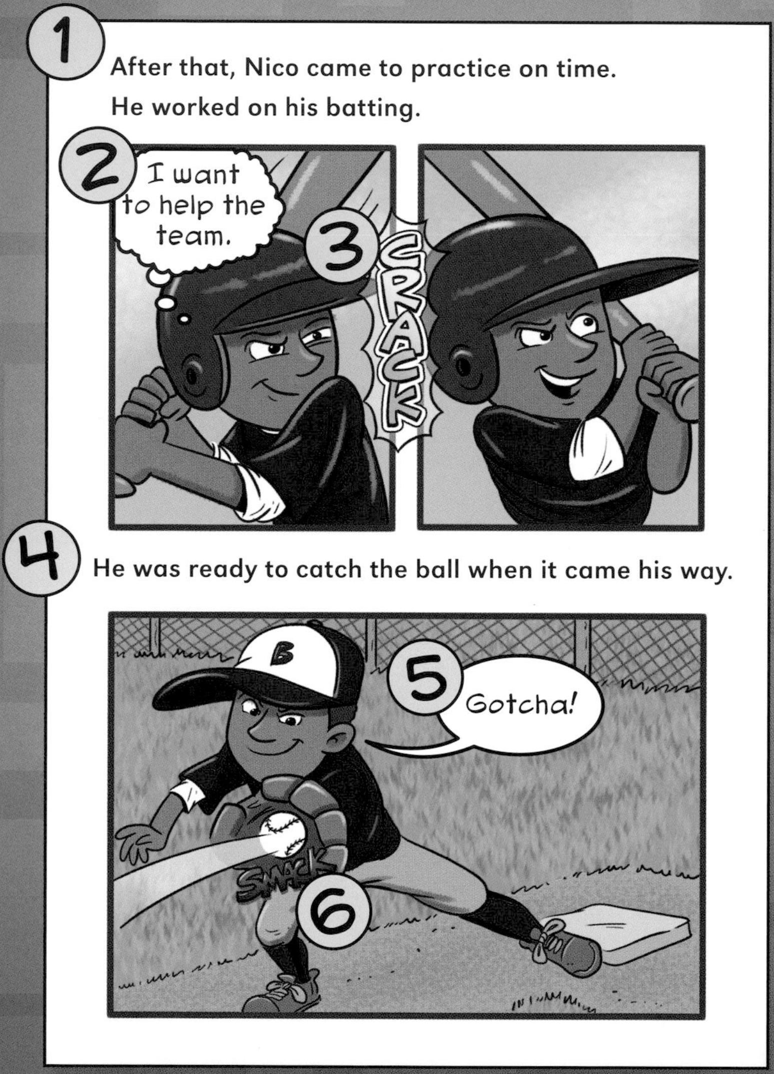

1
After that, Nico came to practice on time.
He worked on his batting.
2
I want to help the team.
3
CRACK
4
He was ready to catch the ball when it came his way.
5
Gotcha!
SMACK
6

The pictures and the words work together to tell the whole story.

Casey did not want to go swimming.

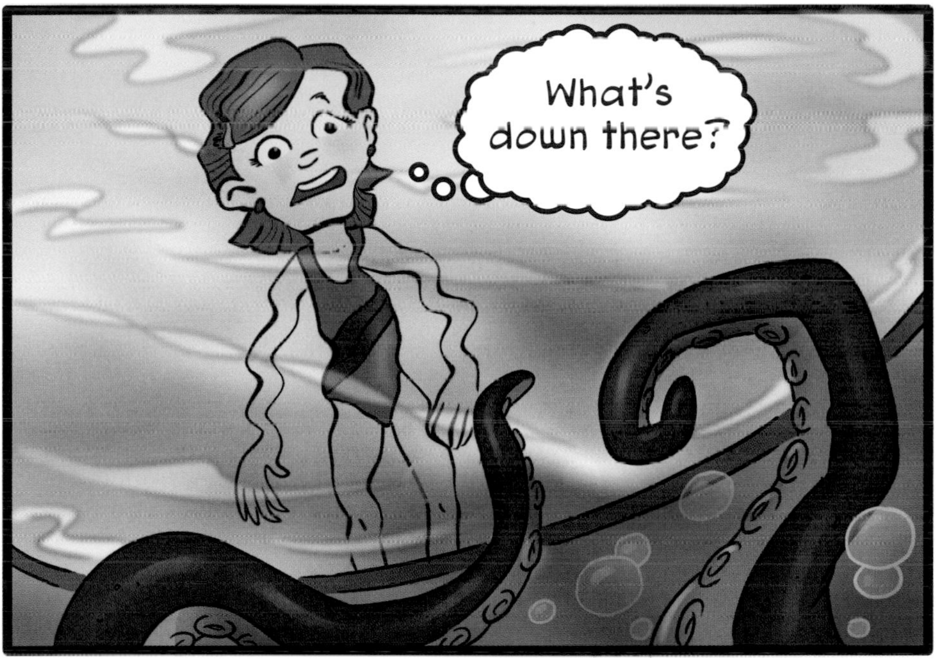
What's down there?

Water might get in her eyes and up her nose.

Her hair would get wet.

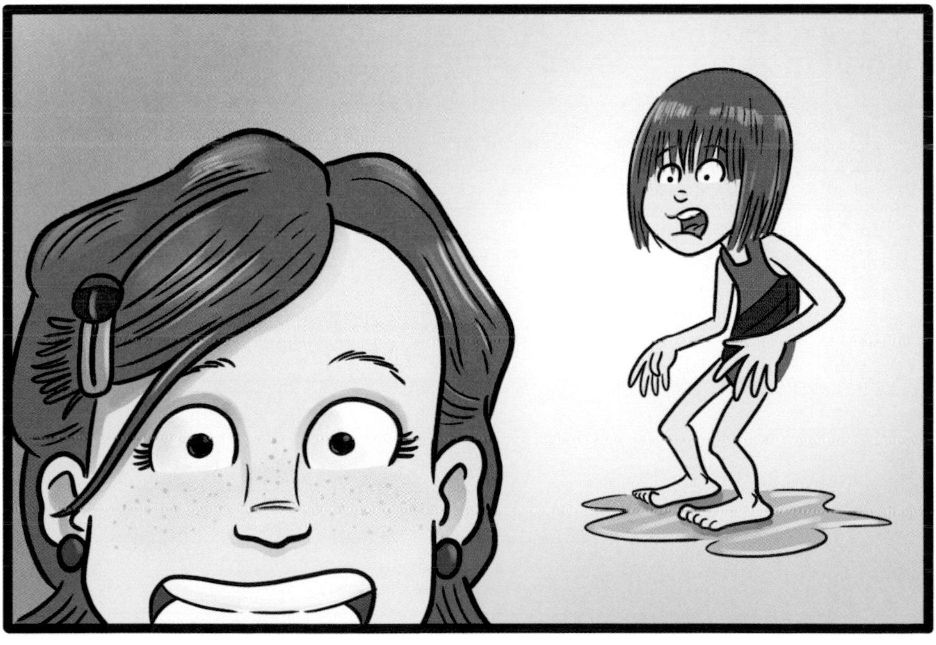

Then Casey saw the new pool at the sports center. It looked so fun.

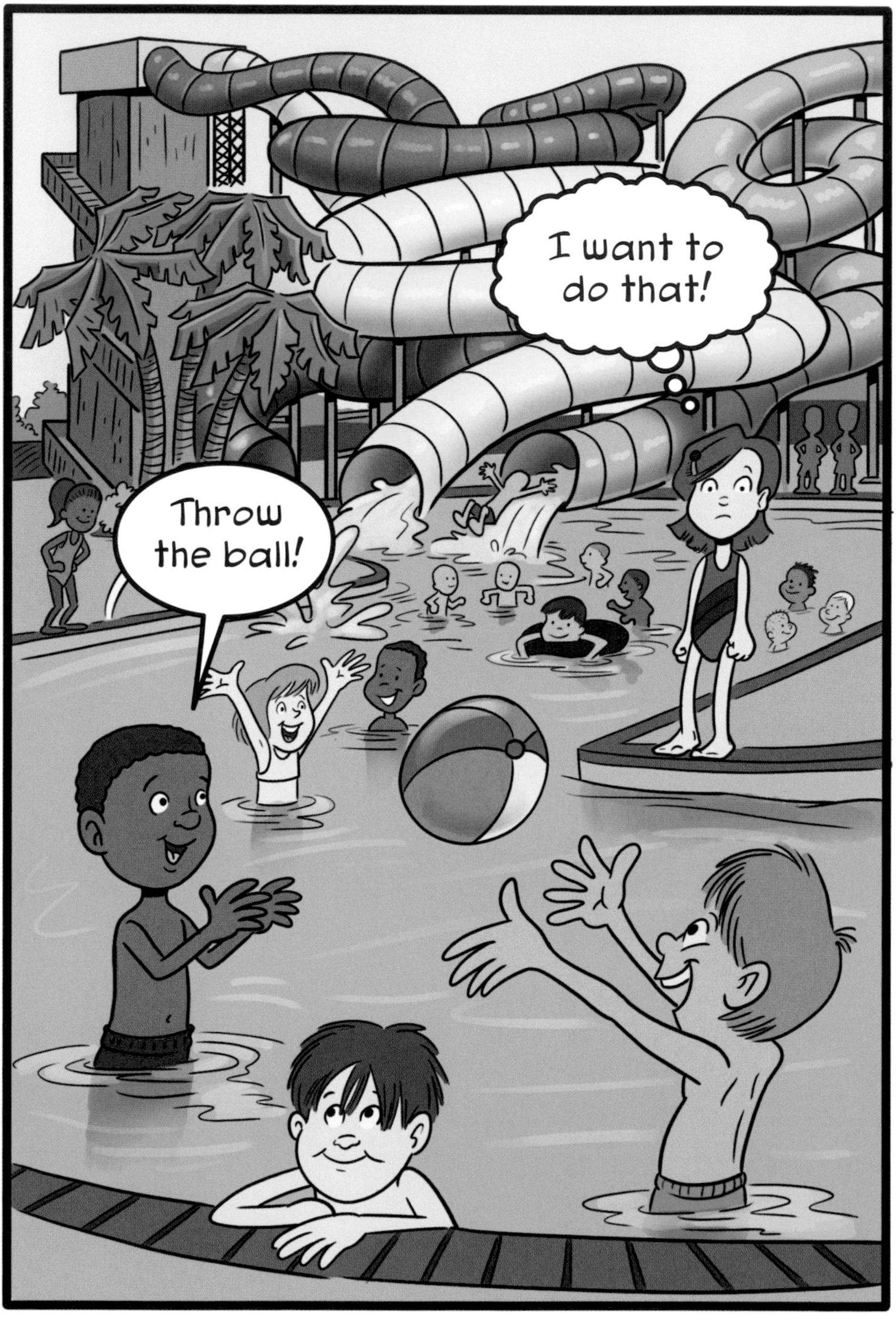
I want to do that!
Throw the ball!

Casey tried out the water playground. A flower rained drops of water. Casey kept going under it.

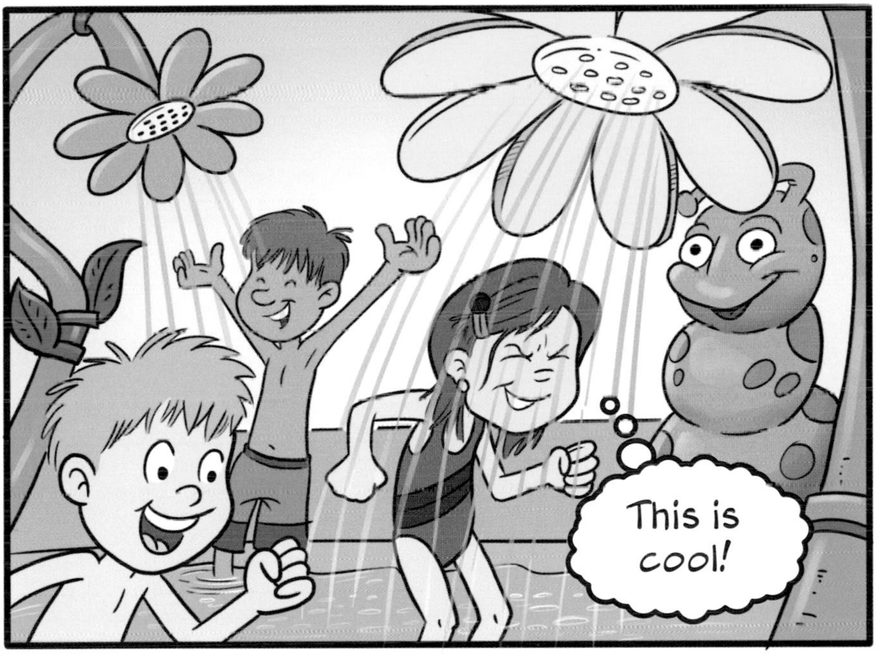
This is cool!

Then she saw her friend Ben.

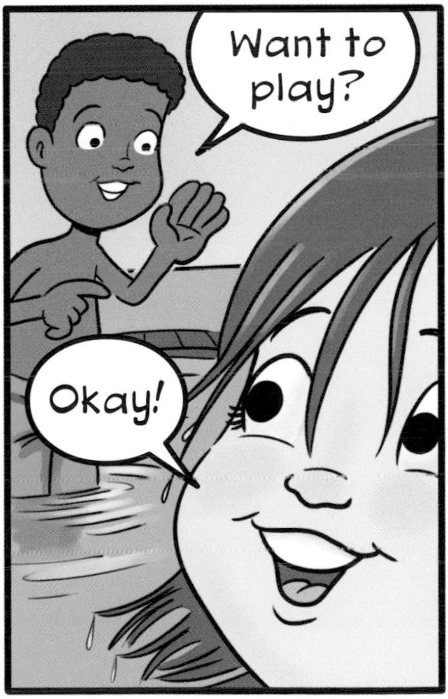
Want to play?
Okay!

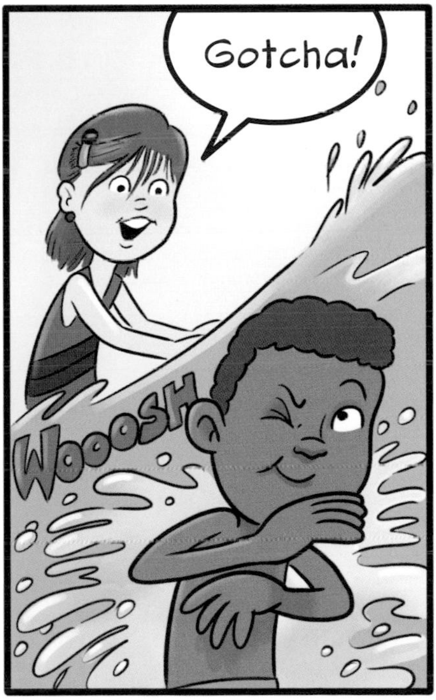
Gotcha!
WOOOSH

Ben wanted to go down the slide. It looked fast and scary to Casey.

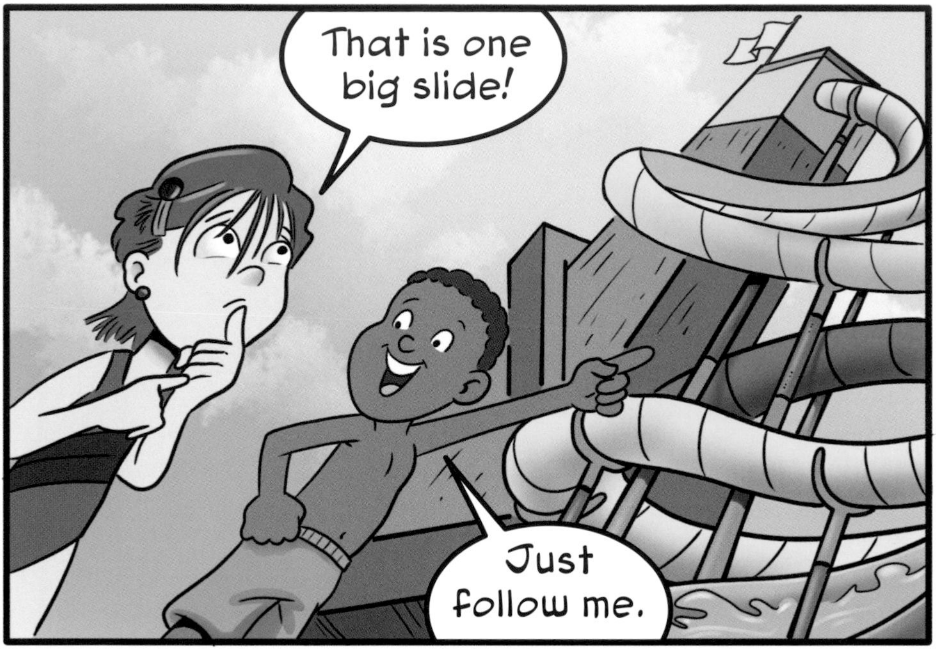
That is one big slide!
Just follow me.

But when she tried it, she thought it was fun!

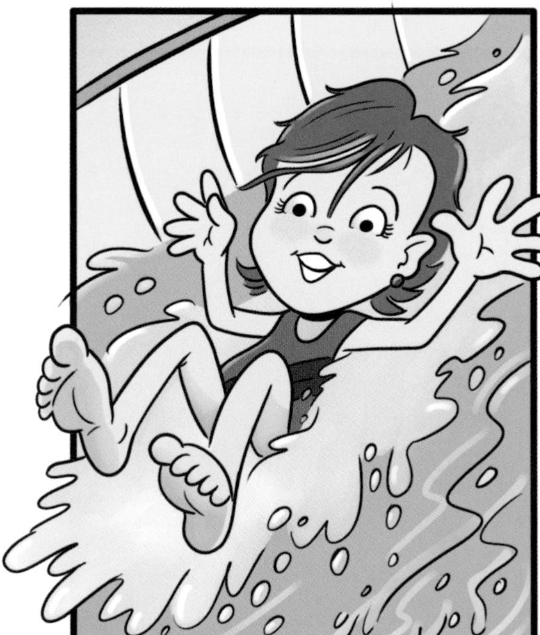

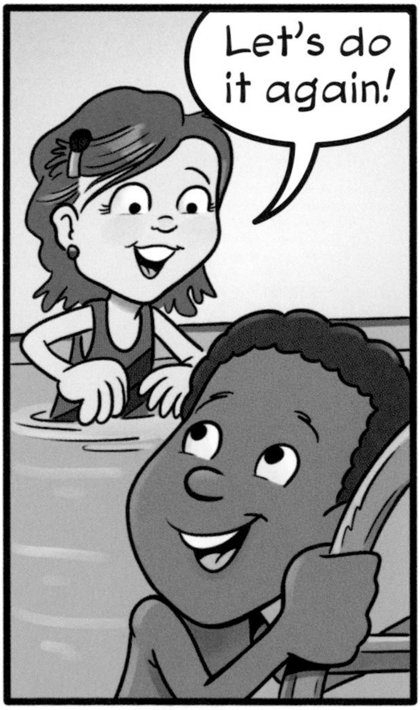
Let's do it again!

After a few more trips to the swim area, Casey loved the water and swimming.

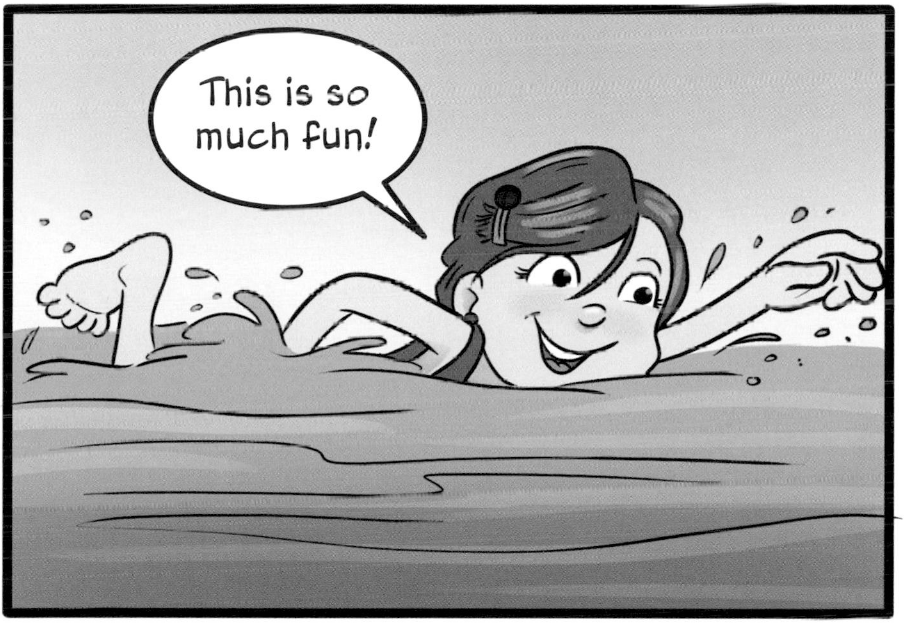
This is so much fun!

Then she had an idea. What would happen if she entered a swim race?

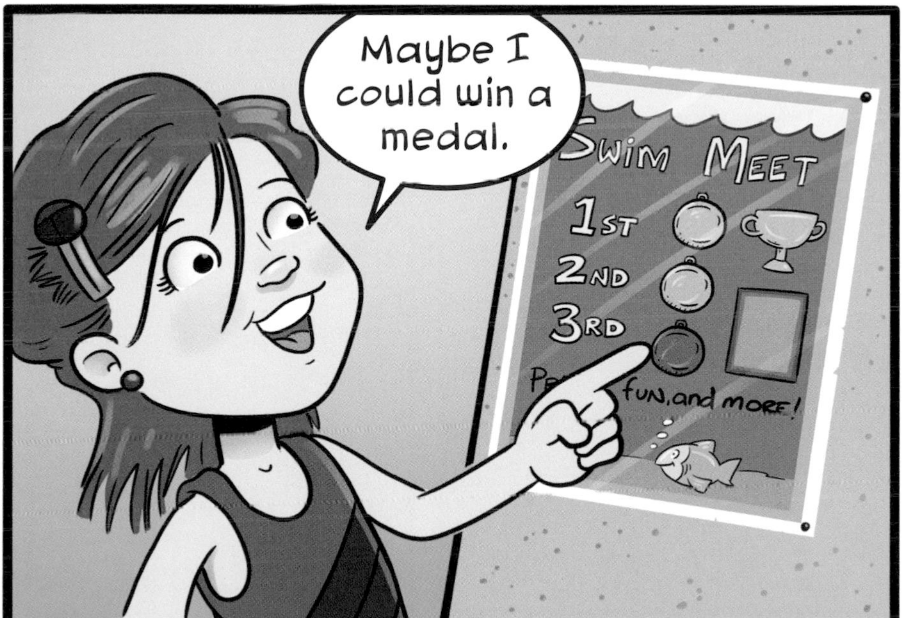
Maybe I could win a medal.
SWIM MEET
1ST
2ND
3RD
FUN, and MORE!

Casey would be nervous on the day of the race.

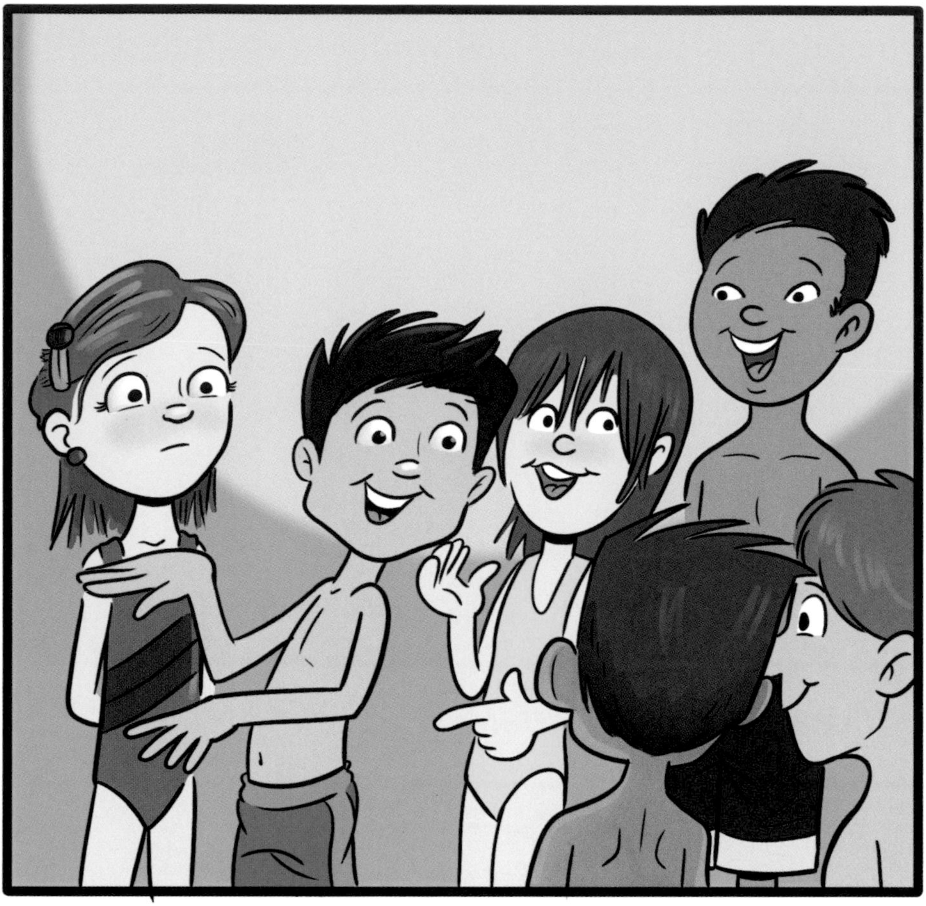

But her friend Ben would make her feel better.

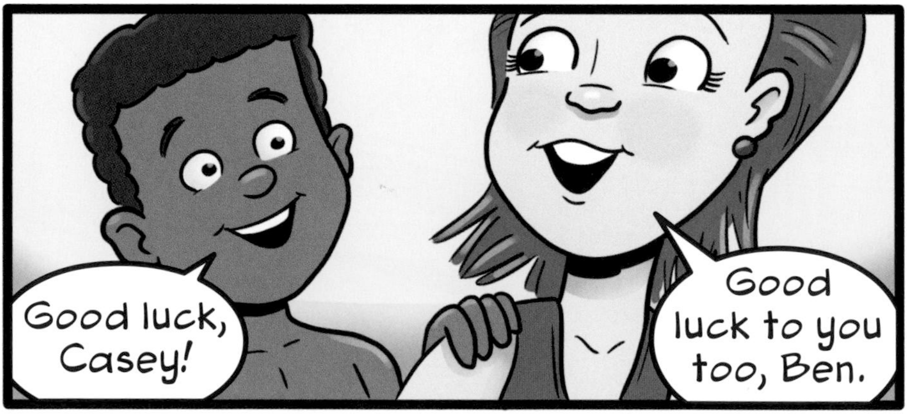
Good luck, Casey!
Good luck to you too, Ben.

Casey would be excited. This race would be just the beginning. Maybe she would be a lifeguard.

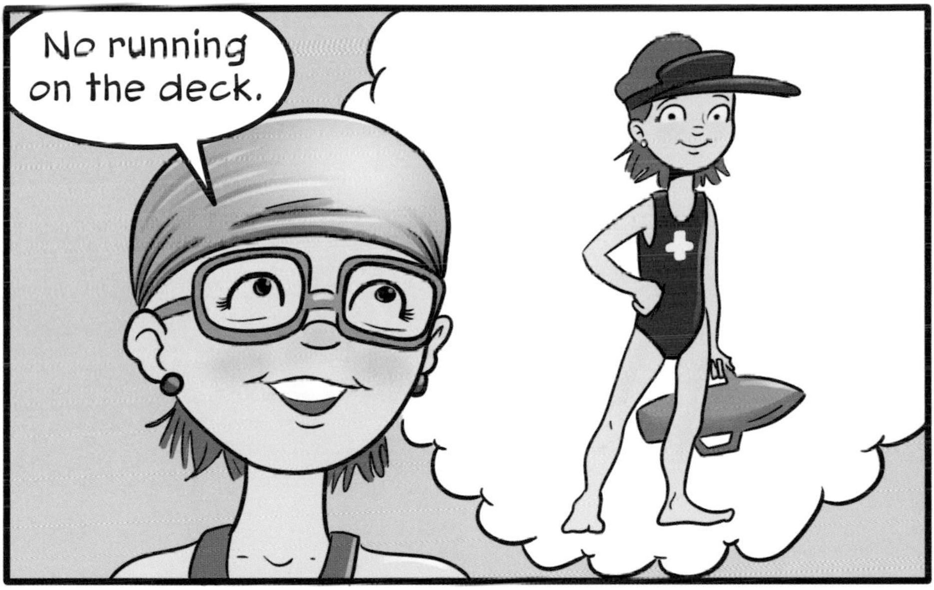
No running on the deck.

Maybe she would surf in the ocean.

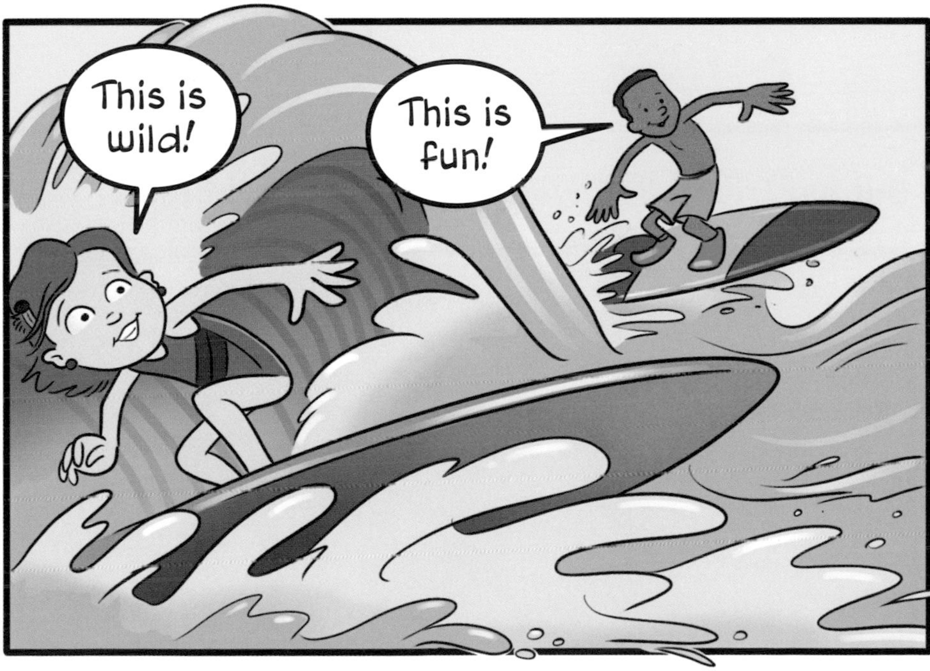
This is wild!
This is fun!

The lifeguard would tell the racers the rules.

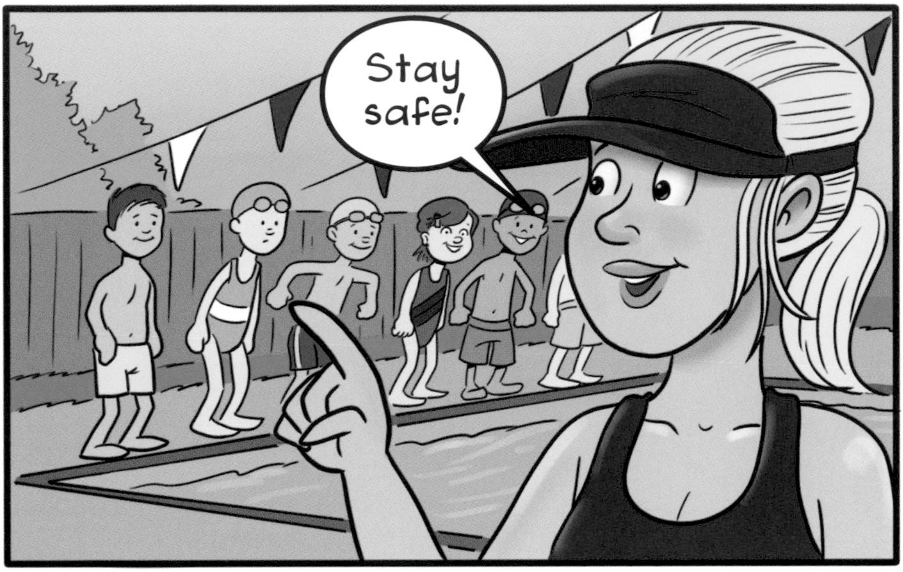
Stay safe!

Casey would put on her swim cap. It would hug her head.

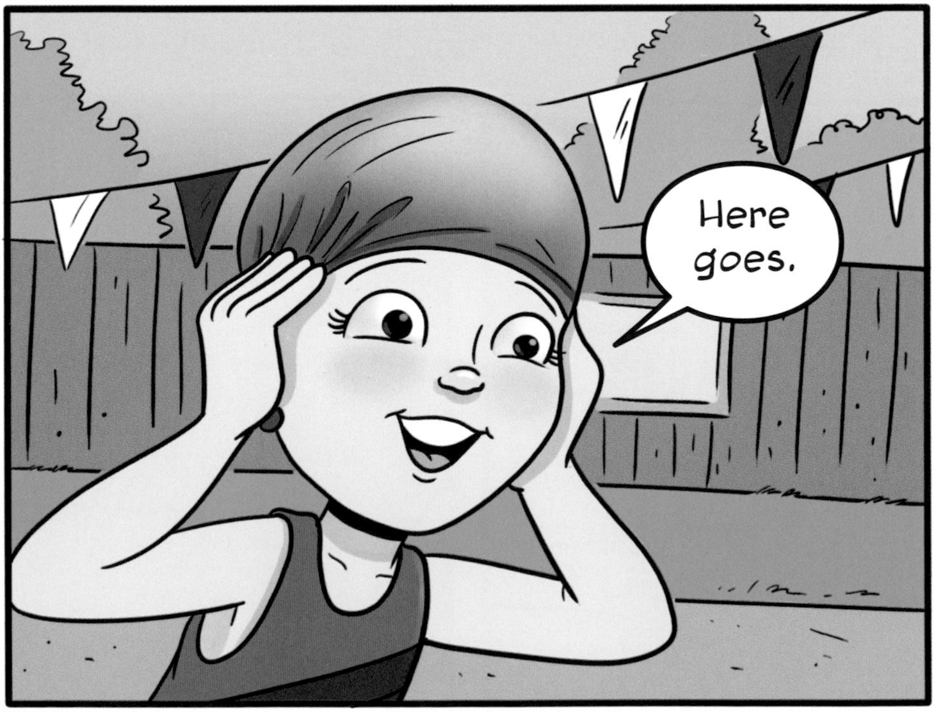
Here goes.

She would get into her lane. The water would be freezing!

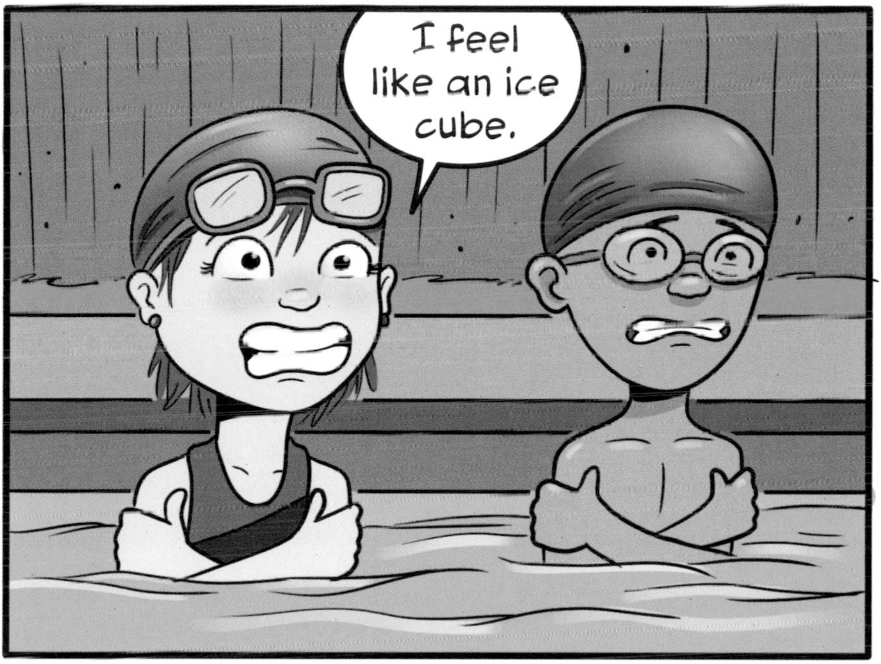
I feel like an ice cube.

She would lower her goggles over her eyes.

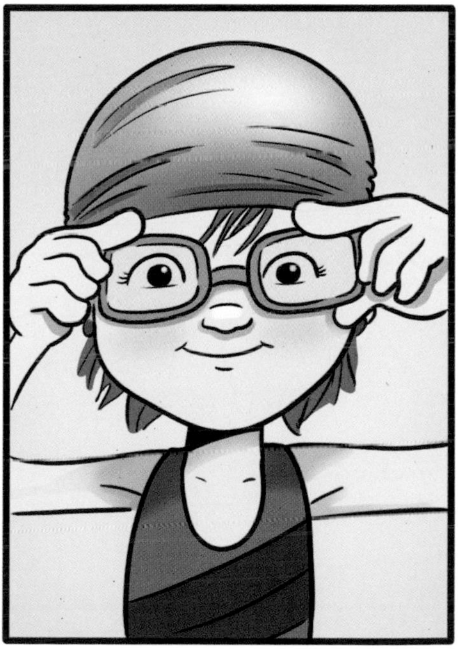

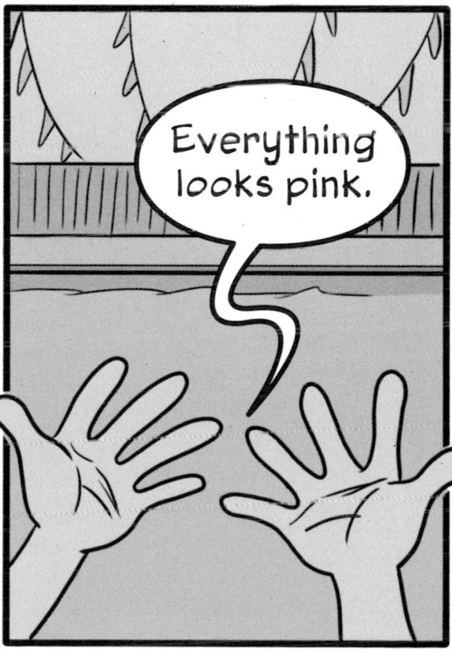
Everything looks pink.

Finally, the whistle would blow. Casey would push off the wall.

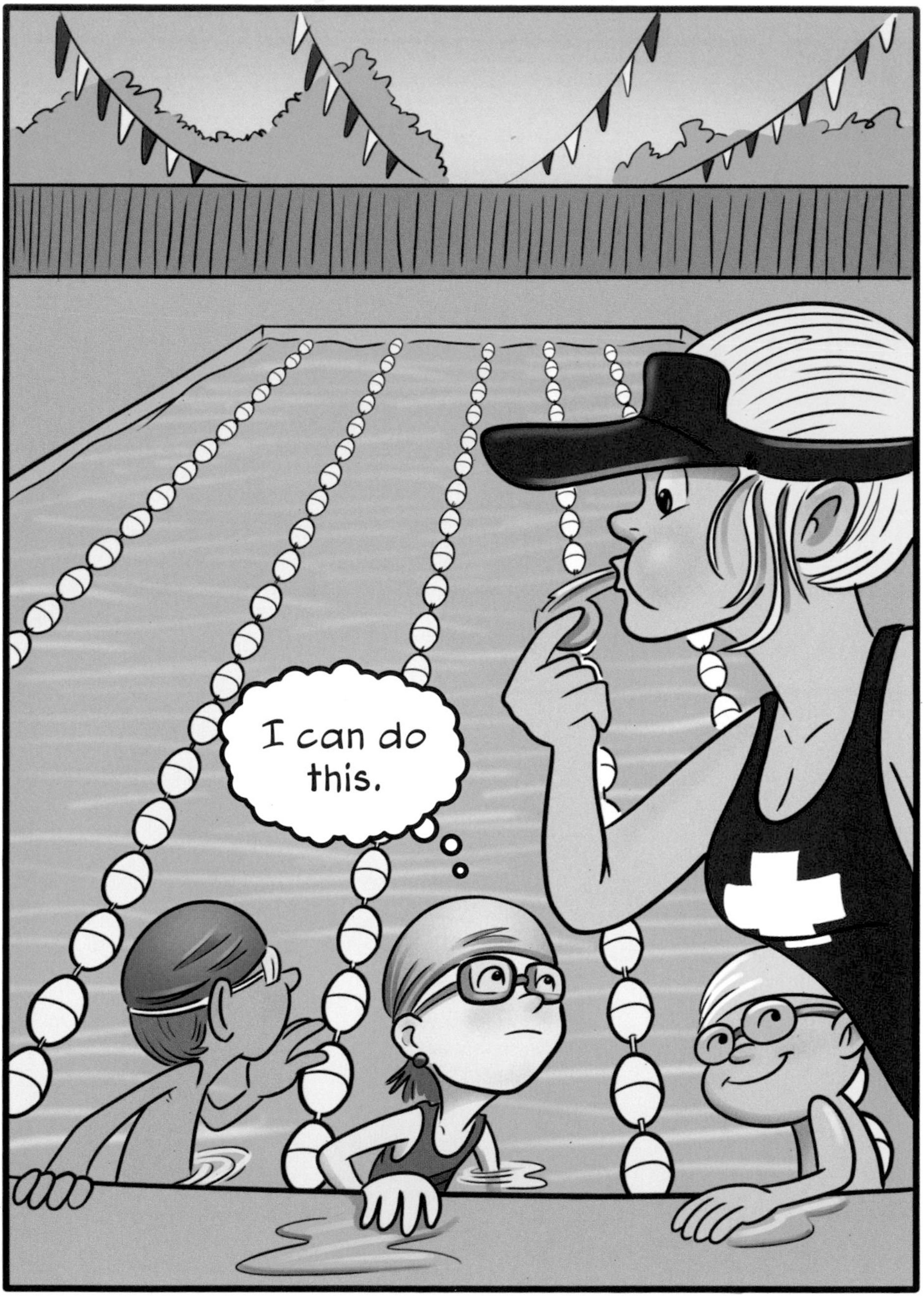
I can do this.

Casey would speed down the pool.

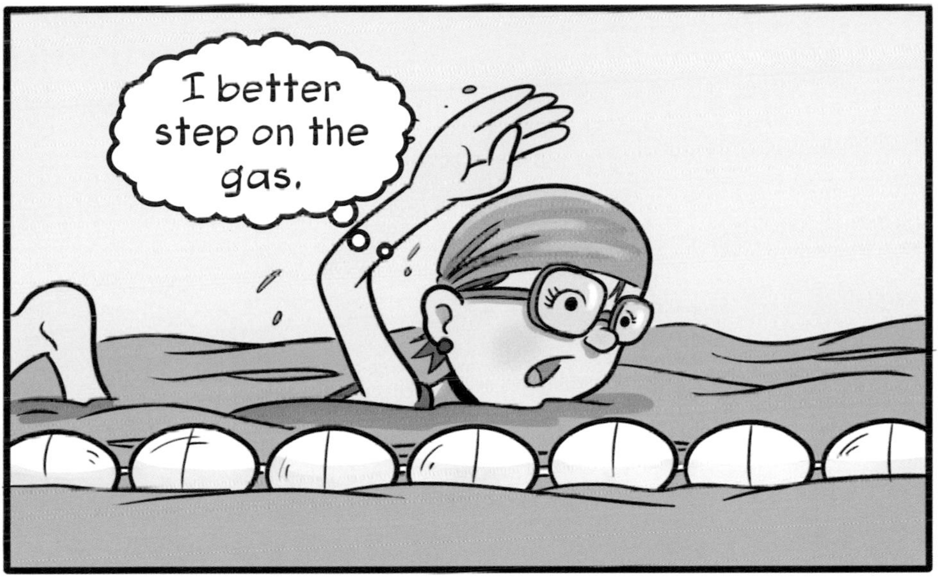
I better step on the gas.

She would swim faster than a dolphin.

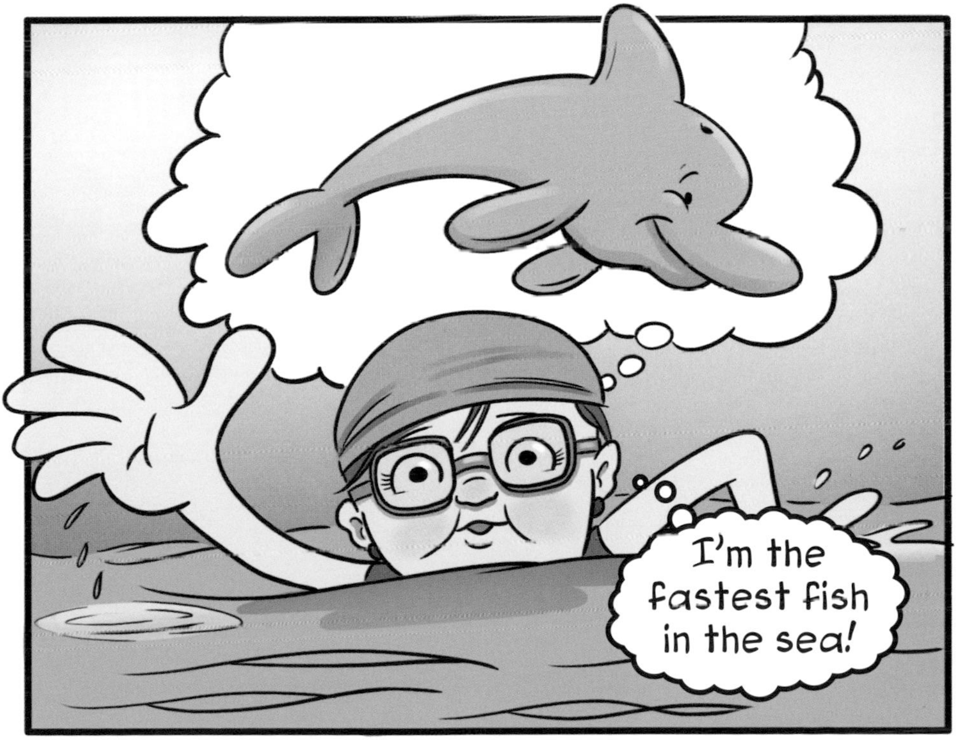
I'm the fastest fish in the sea!

Her legs would go up and down like scissors.

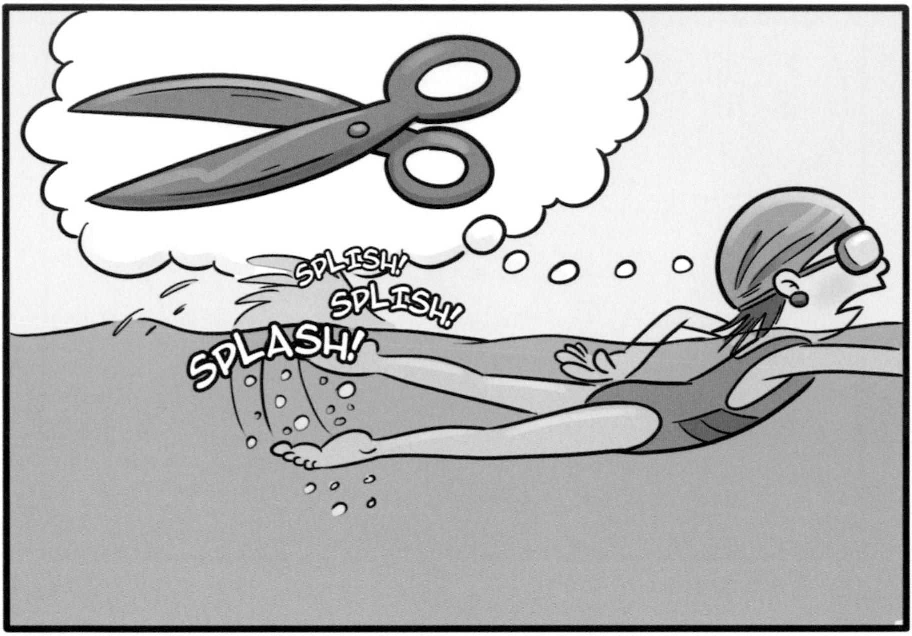
SPLISH!
SPLISH!
SPLASH!

Her arms would go round and round like a windmill.

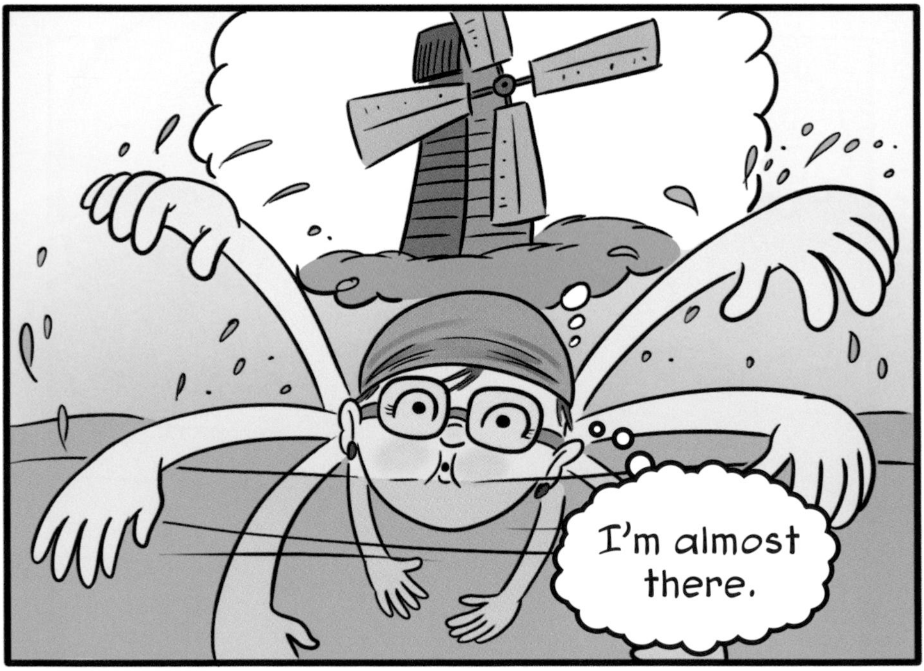
I'm almost there.

Wave after wave would wash over her.

Casey might swallow some water.

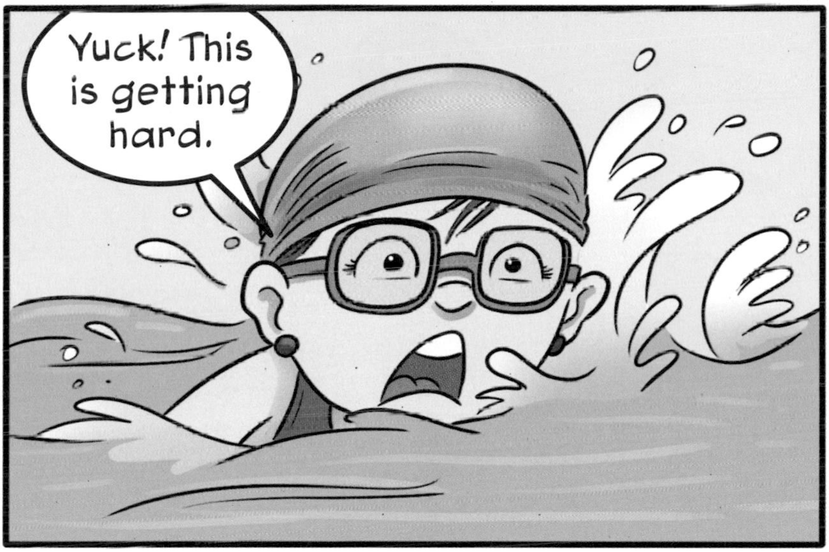
Yuck! This is getting hard.

Her goggles might fill with water!

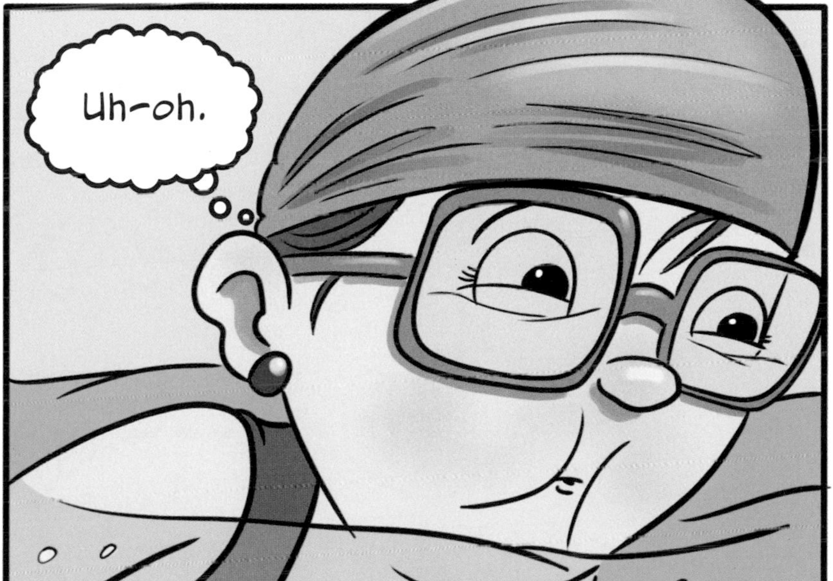
Uh-oh.

But Casey would keep swimming.

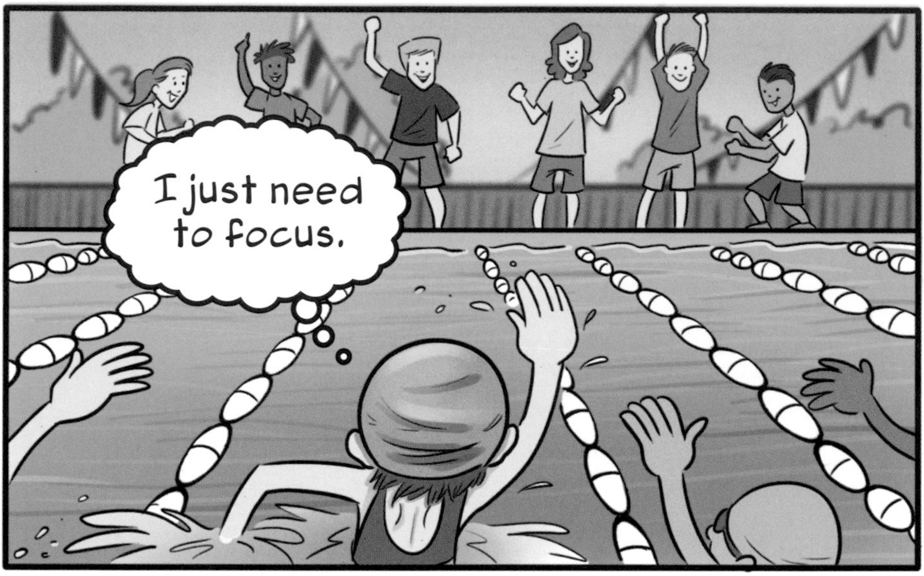
I just need to focus.

She would turn her head this way to breathe in.
She would turn her head that way to breathe out.

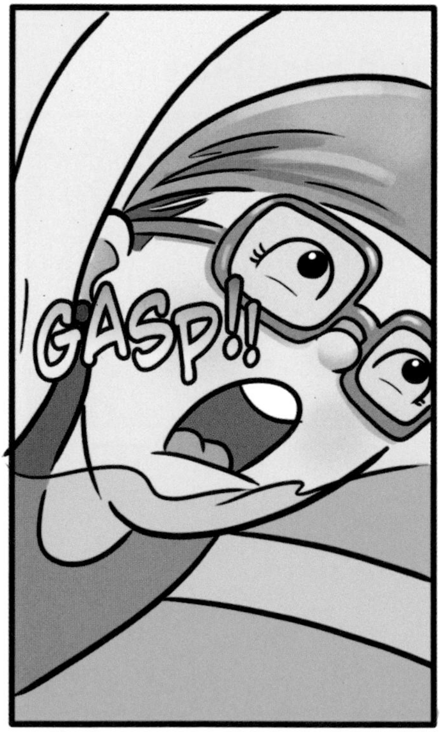
GASP!!

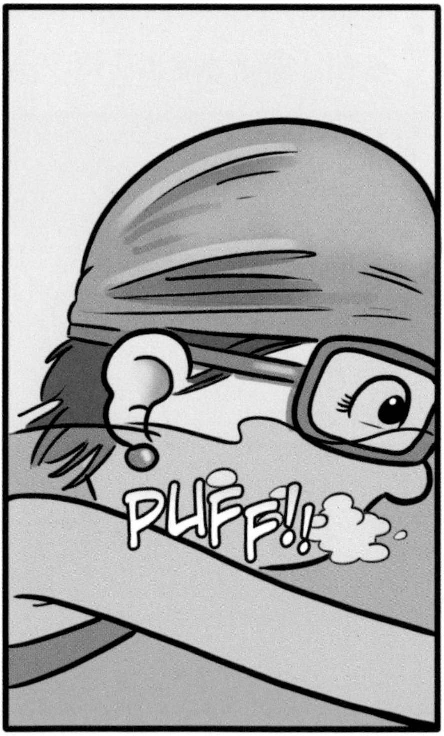
PUFF!!

Casey would swim faster and faster. She would pass her friend Ben.

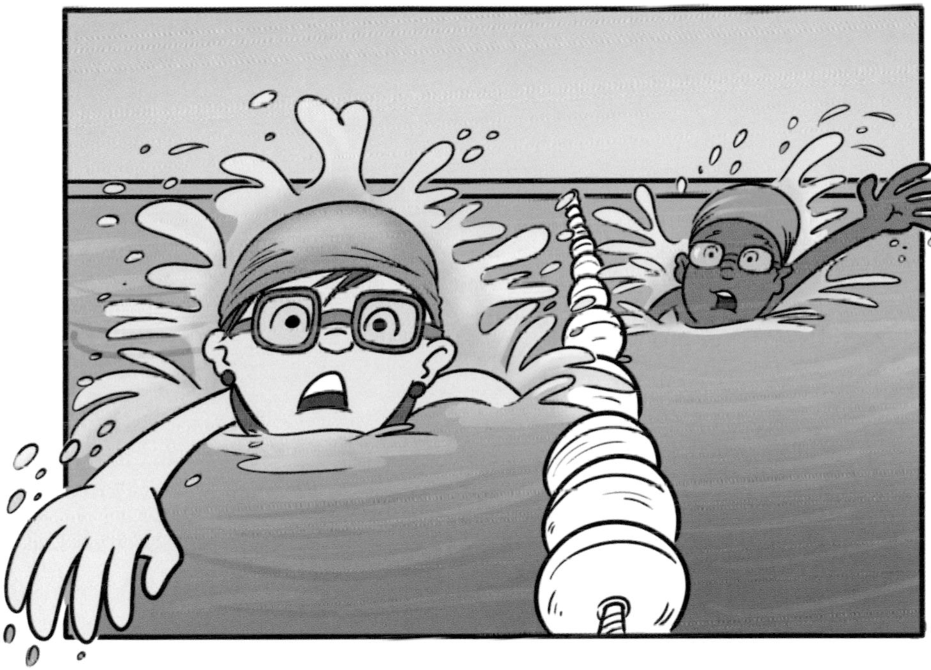

Casey would tuck her knees and feet in at the wall. She would flip over and head back.

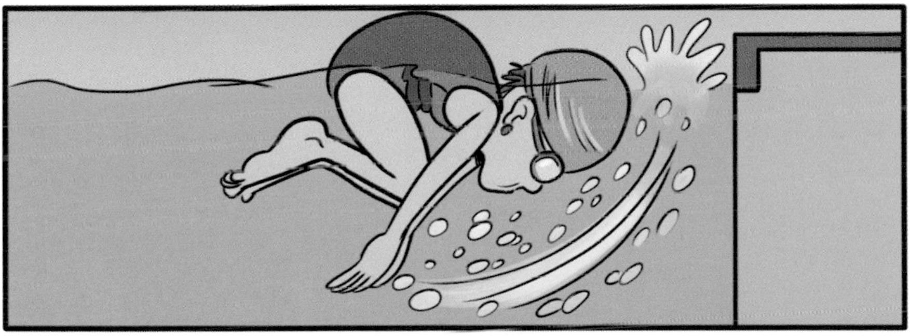

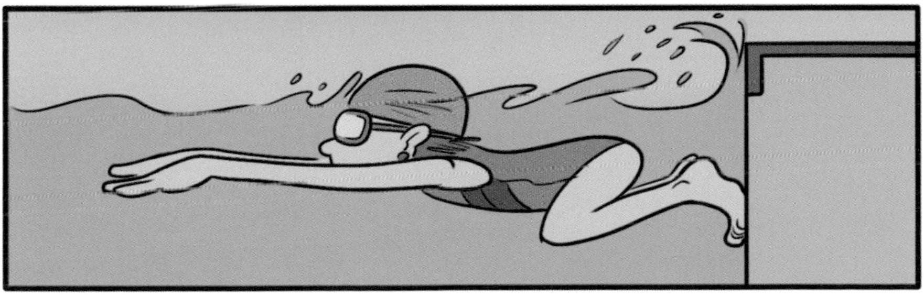

The crowd would roar loudly. Casey would kick toward the finish.

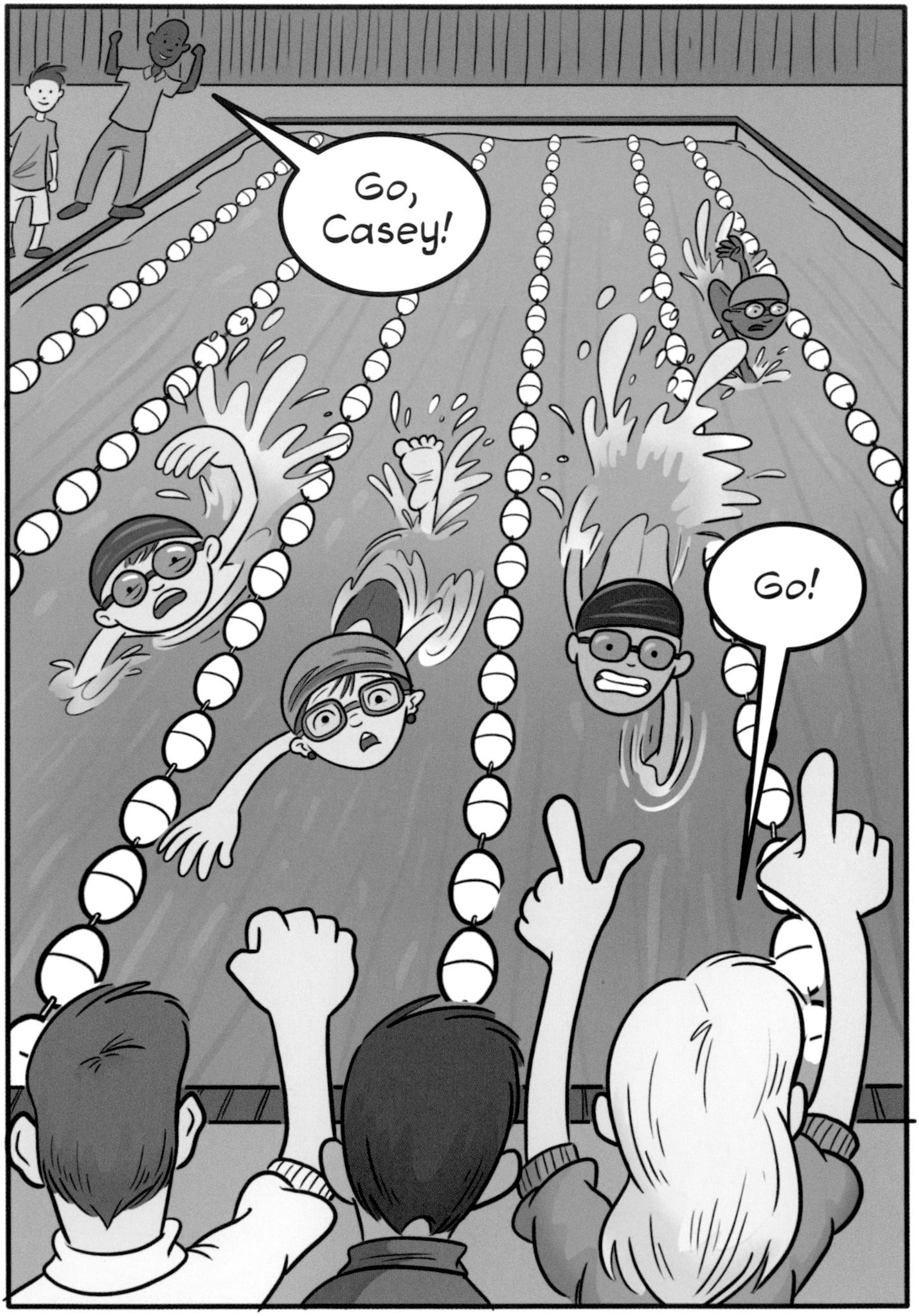
Go, Casey!
Go!

Casey would grab the edge. She would win!

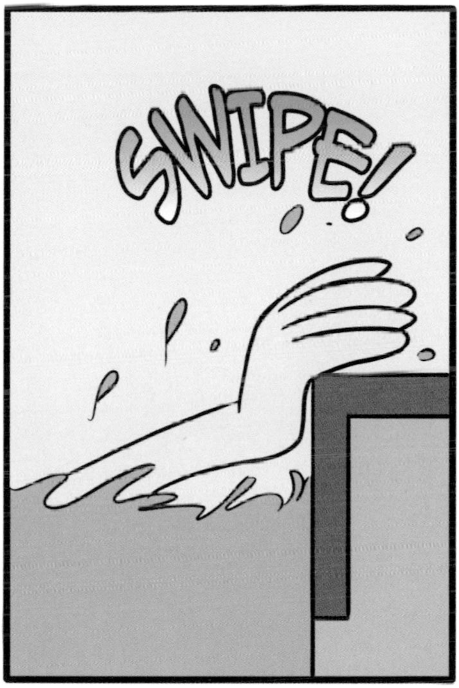
SWIPE!

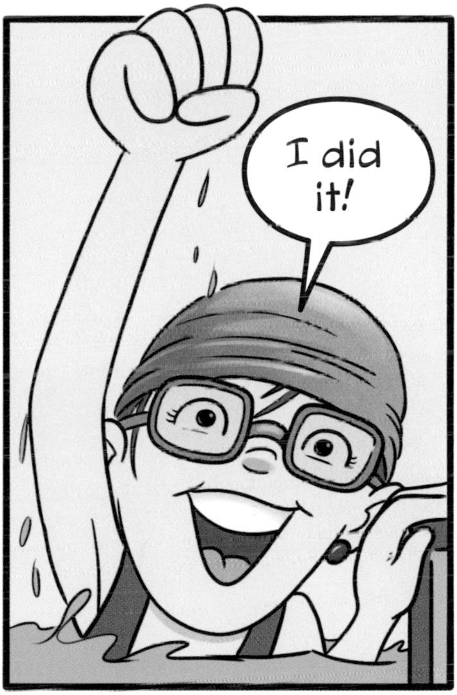
I did it!

When she climbed up the ladder, her mom would give her a big hug.

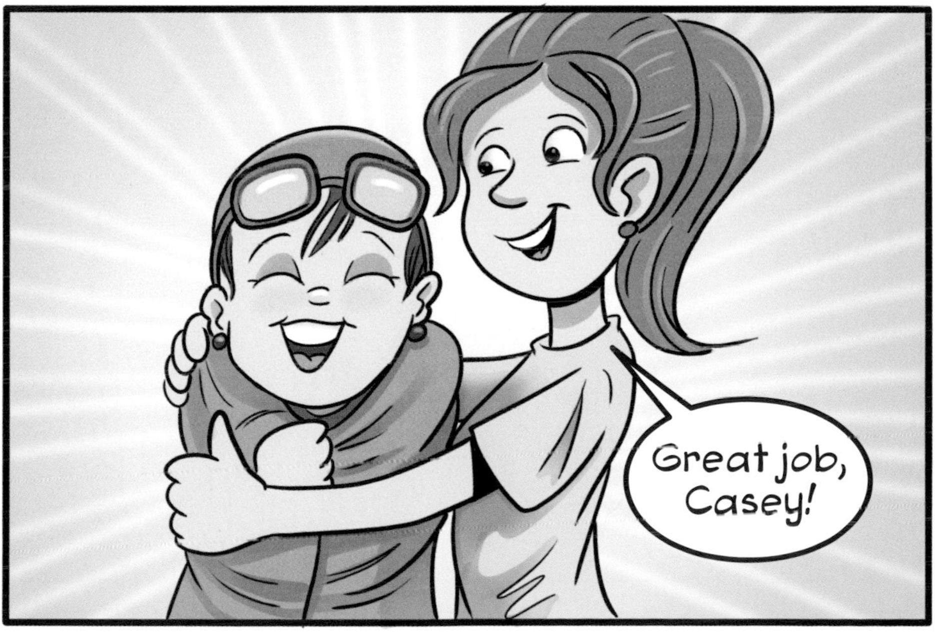
Great job, Casey!

After the race, Casey would get a trophy.

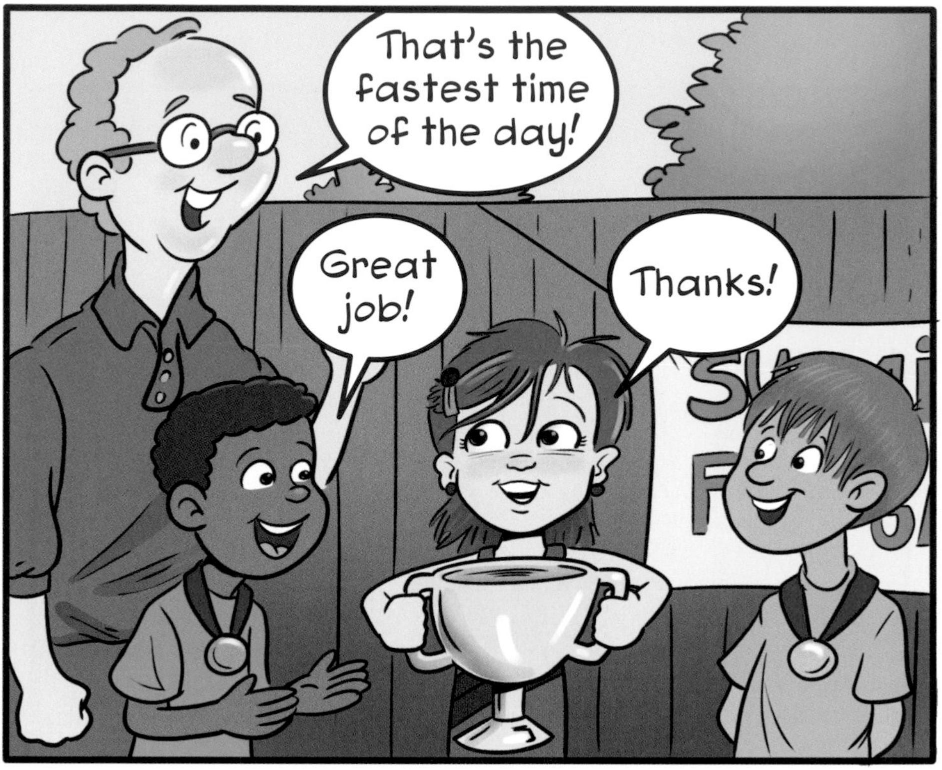
That's the fastest time of the day!
Great job!
Thanks!

She would be so happy.

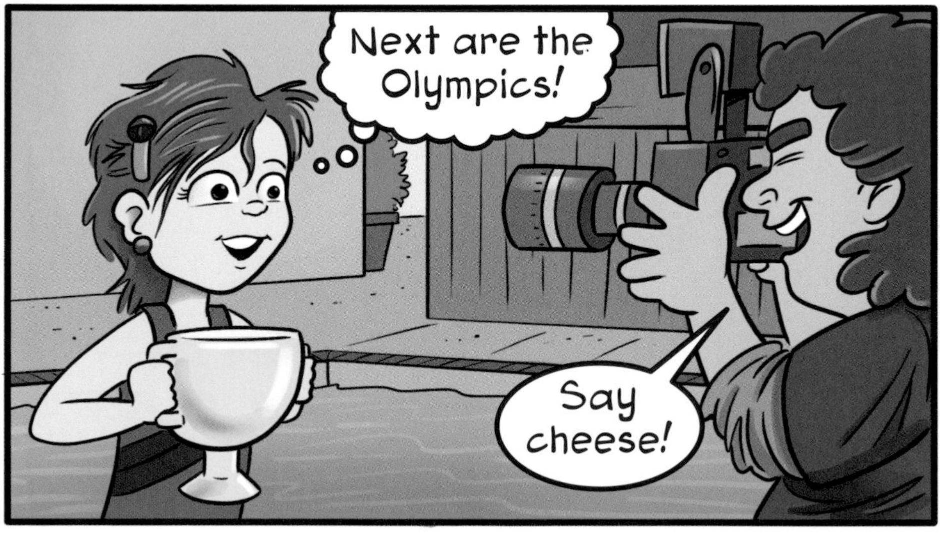
Next are the Olympics!
Say cheese!

But that was all just a dream. For now, she would keep working on her breathing.

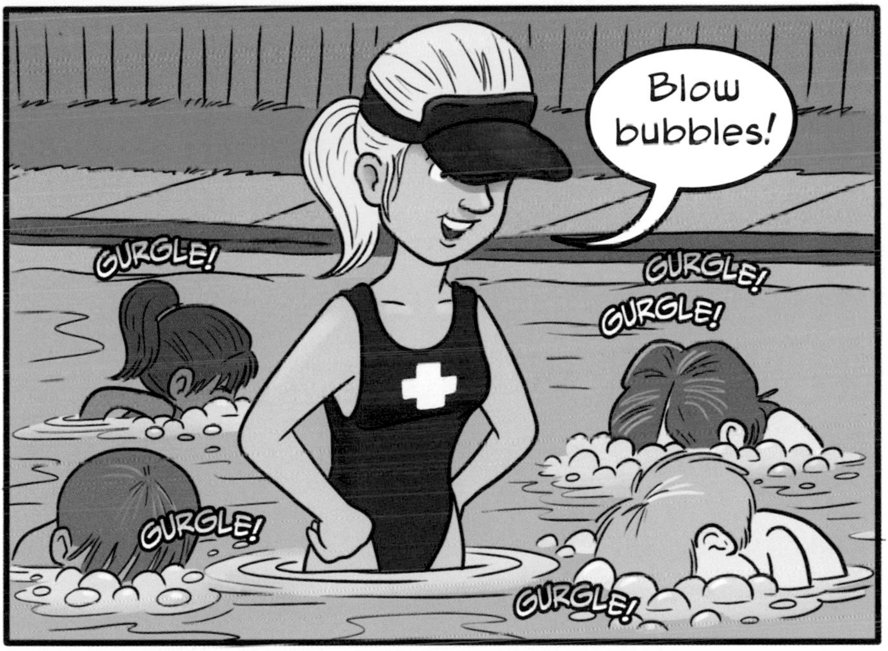
Blow bubbles!
GURGLE!
GURGLE!
GURGLE!
GURGLE!
GURGLE!

She would keep working on her arms.

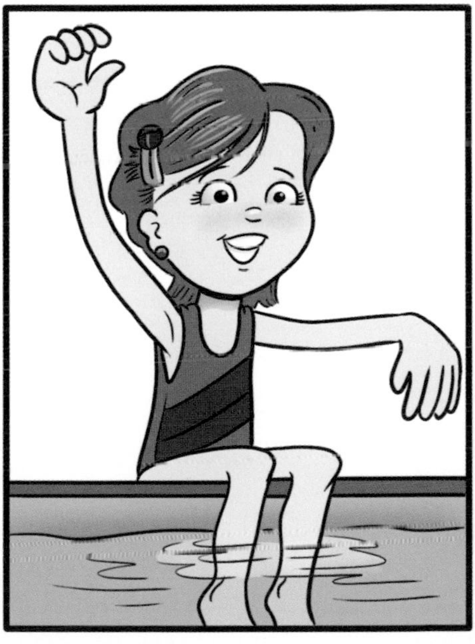

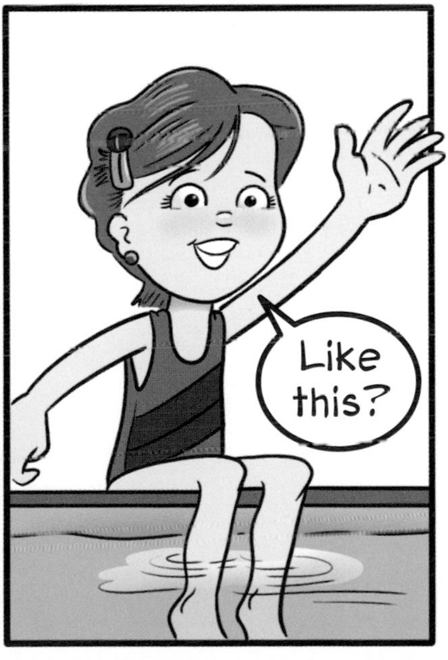
Like this?

She would keep working on her kicks.

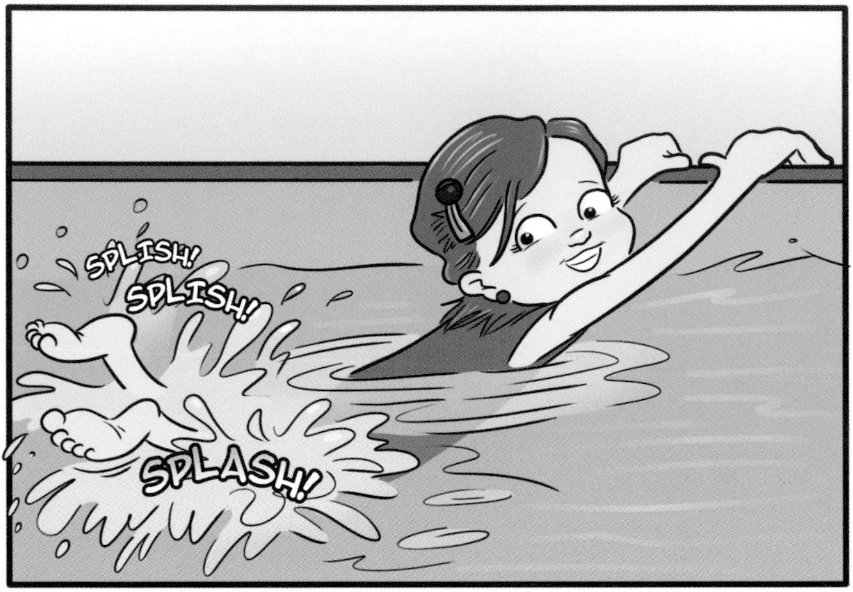
SPLISH!
SPLISH!
SPLASH!

And at her next lesson, she might even let go of the wall!

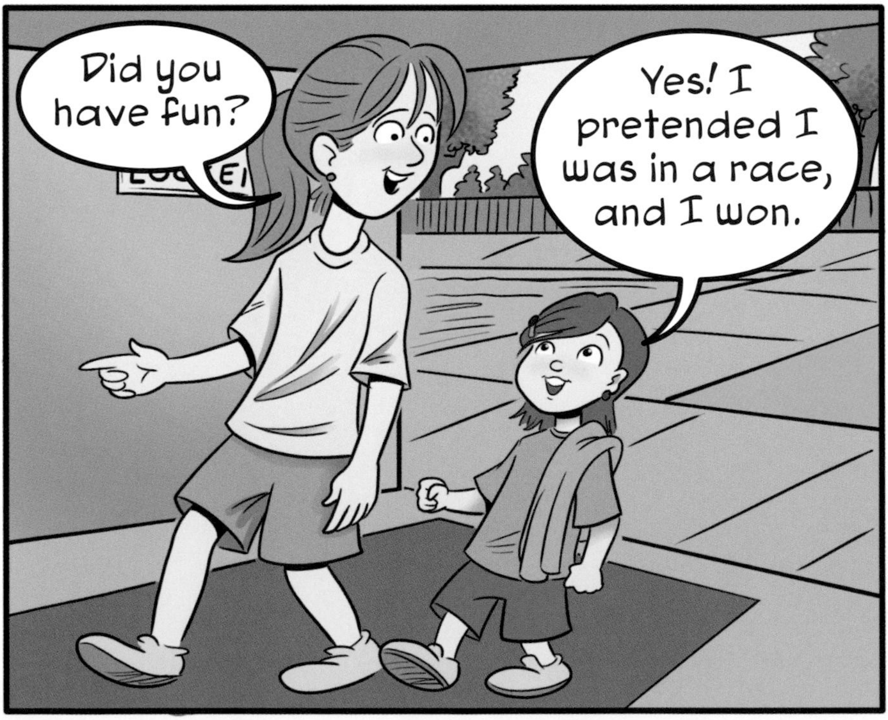
Did you have fun?
Yes! I pretended I was in a race, and I won.

BIOGRAPHIES

ANITA YASUDA lives in a small town with her husband, daughter, and dog, Ted. When she is not writing, she enjoys musical theater, Pilates, skiing, and walking Ted. While Ted is happy to just chase squirrels, Anita and her daughter love to travel. They have been on more than 100 trips and hope to visit every continent some day.

STEVE HARPSTER has loved drawing funny cartoons, mean monsters, and goofy gadgets since he was able to pick up a pencil. Now he does it for a living. Steve lives in Columbus, Ohio, with his wonderful wife, Karen, and their sheepdog, Doodle.

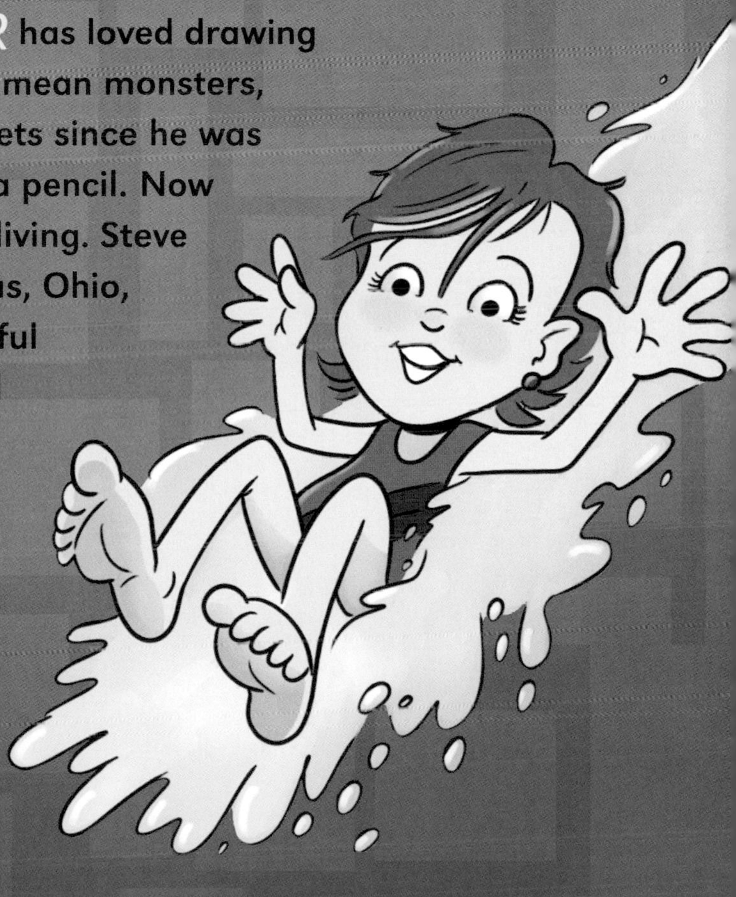

GLOSSARY

EXCITED (ek-SITE-ed) — feeling eager and interested

FOCUS (FOH-kuhss) — to think hard about something

GOGGLES (GOG-uhlz) — special glasses that fit tightly around your eyes to protect them

LIFEGUARD (LIFE-gard) — someone who is trained to save swimmers in danger

SCISSORS (SIZ-urz) — a sharp tool with two blades used for cutting paper, fabric, etc.

TROPHY (TROH-fee) — a prize or an award given to a winning athlete or team or someone who has done something outstanding

WHISTLE (WISS-uhl) — an instrument that makes a high, shrill, loud sound when you blow it

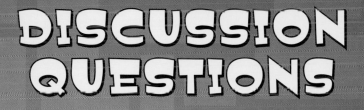

DISCUSSION QUESTIONS

1. Casey had to work hard at swimming. What is something you have worked hard at?

2. In the book, Casey imagines herself in a swim race. Have you ever imagined yourself doing something? What was it?

3. Have you ever taken swimming lessons? What did you like about them? What did you not like?

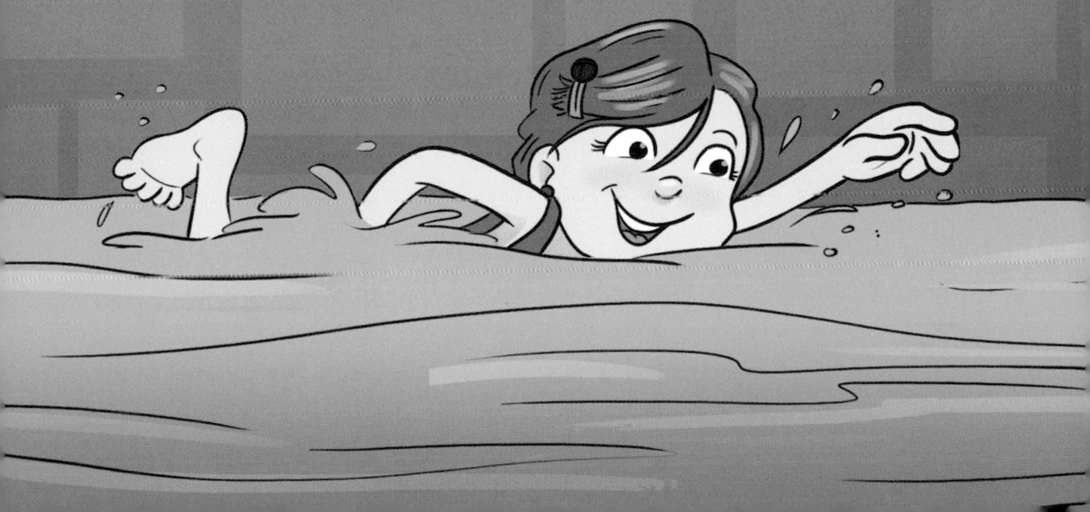

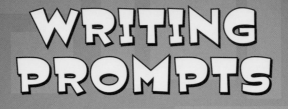

WRITING PROMPTS

1. If you could be in a race, what type of race would it be? Write a few sentences about it.

2. The pool is an exciting place to visit. Draw three things you see at a pool. Label your picture.

3. In the book, there are sound and action words next to some of the pictures. Pick at least two of those words. Then write your own sentences using those words.

MY FIRST GRAPHIC NOVEL

These books are the perfect introduction to the world of safe, appealing graphic novels. Each story uses familiar topics, repeating patterns, and core vocabulary words appropriate for a beginning reader. Combine the entertaining story with comic book panels, exciting action elements, and bright colors and a safe graphic novel is born.

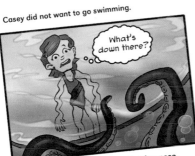

Casey did not want to go swimming.
What's down there?
Water might get in her eyes and up her nose. Her hair would get wet.
6
Then Casey saw the new pool at the sports center. It looked so fun.
I want to do that!
Throw the ball.
7

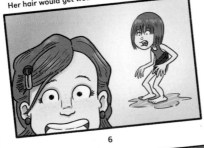

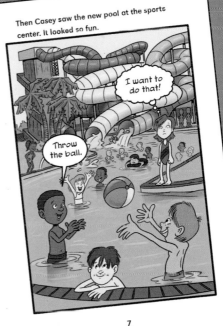

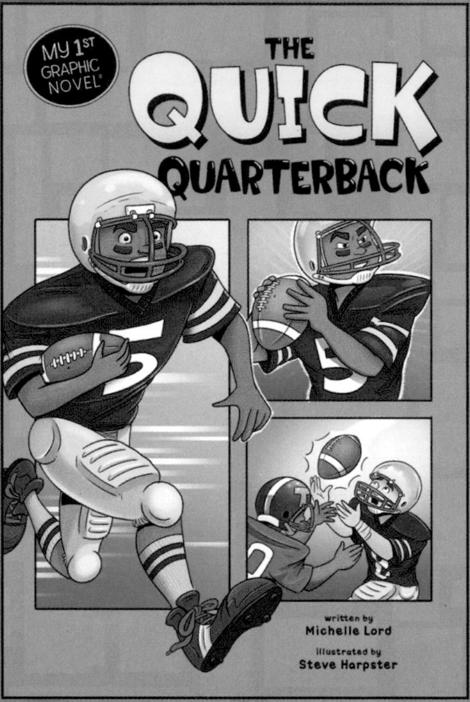
MY 1ST GRAPHIC NOVEL
THE QUICK QUARTERBACK
written by
Michelle Lord
illustrated by
Steve Harpster

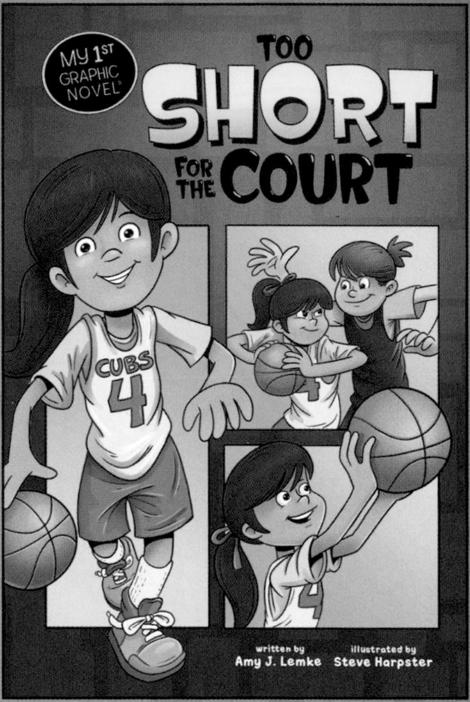
MY 1ST GRAPHIC NOVEL
TOO SHORT FOR THE COURT
CUBS 4
written by
Amy J. Lemke
illustrated by
Steve Harpster

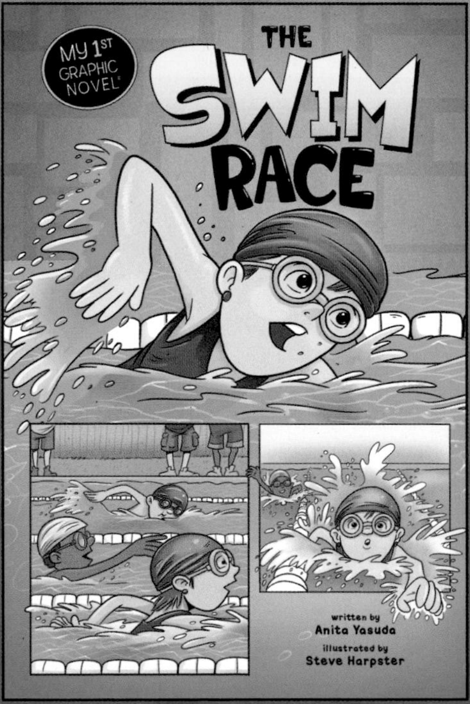
MY 1ST GRAPHIC NOVEL
THE SWIM RACE
written by
Anita Yasuda
illustrated by
Steve Harpster

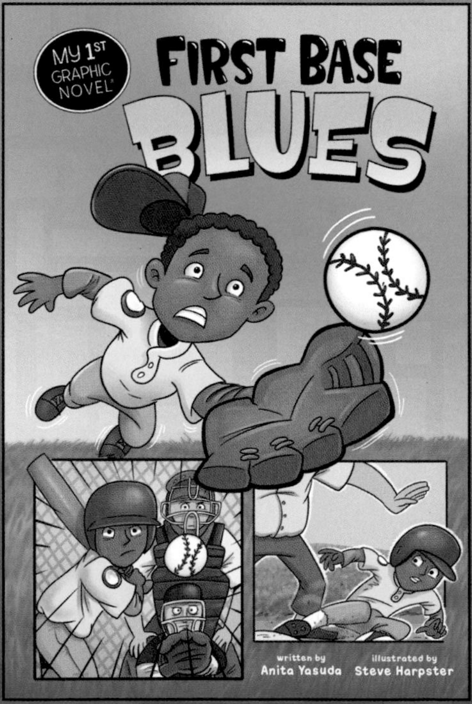
MY 1ST GRAPHIC NOVEL
FIRST BASE BLUES
written by
Anita Yasuda
illustrated by
Steve Harpster